To Mati ♡ ...

Stay A WESOME!

ANYTHING
BUT ORDINARY

The Beginning

Kayla M. Hebbon

Kayla M. Hebbon ♡

ISBN 978-0-9987769-0-3 (Paperback Edition)
ISBN 978-0-9987769-1-0 (EPUB Edition)

Library of Congress Control Number: 2018901747

Copy Edited by Helen M. Gocher
Cover Design by Tim Bland

Printed and bound in USA
First Printing January 2018

Published by Kay Kay Publishing, LLC
19 Clyde Road, Suite 202
Somerset, NJ 08873

To my mother, Kisha M. Hebbon, Esq.

Contents

1

Another Day

Julie woke up to the sound of her alarm clock. She sat up and turned the clock off. Julie then got out of bed and walked out of her room to the bathroom door. She tried to open it, but it was locked. She knew her little brother, Justin, was in the bathroom.

"Justin, open the door!" she shouted, knocking on the door.

"Sorry. I can't open it at the moment," Justin said from the bathroom.

"Why not?" Julie asked him.

"I was doing an experiment and it had an unfortunate chemical reaction. So now I'm cleaning it up," Justin explained.

Justin was a very smart boy for his age. He was eight years old and already in the sixth grade. He was always doing homework or science experiments around the house, so this was normal for Julie.

"Well, how am I supposed to use the bathroom?" Julie asked.

"You can use the downstairs bathroom for now," Justin said.

"Fine. Well, can I at least have my toothbrush?" Julie asked. Justin opened the door a crack and stuck his hand through the door. Julie's toothbrush was in his hand.

"Thanks," Julie said as she took it from him. Justin closed the door. "Wait. I forgot about toothpaste," she said. Justin opened the door and handed her the toothpaste tube. "Thanks. You might want to hurry up with that mess because you've got a bus to catch," she told him. Julie could now see into the bathroom and saw that most of the floor was covered in some kind of orange liquid.

"Thanks, sis." Justin then closed the door.

Julie brushed her teeth in the downstairs

Chapter 1

bathroom and finished getting ready for school. She went into her bedroom, looked into the mirror, and brushed her hair. Julie had on a pair of jeans, black leather boots, a light-green tank top, and a purple hoodie. She finished brushing her long, golden-brown hair and put the brush down on the dresser. Julie looked at herself in the mirror. "Another day, another seven hours of school with Crystie," she said to herself.

Crystie was Julie's bully. She always called her "shy girl" and picked on her for no reason. Julie was a nice and sweet person, but she was also very shy. That's why Crystie, as well as the other kids at school, called her "shy girl" all the time.

Julie never told anyone about Crystie because she was too shy and she didn't want to get anyone in trouble. Not telling anyone never seemed to bother her much. "At least I have one thing to look forward to: watching Alex Raymond ride his skateboard to school," she said. Julie secretly liked Alex. Every weekday, she would see him riding his skateboard on his way to school. Luckily, Alex never noticed her when she walked across the street from him.

Sometimes, when she watched him ride his skateboard, she got a little distracted. One time, she was so distracted that she tripped on the sidewalk and fell onto a bush. She never talked to him before, and Alex had never talked to her either. But she still enjoyed seeing him at school every weekday. Julie picked up her backpack and left the room.

***

Meanwhile, at Lia's house, Lia was in her room brushing her hair. Well, sort of. She was using her hairbrush as a microphone, singing along to a song playing on her phone. Lia had brown hair with pink highlights that she liked to wear in pigtails. She also loved the color pink. You could probably tell by the color of her hair and her bedroom. Almost everything in Lia's room was pink.

"Lia, hurry up! You're going to be late for school!" her mom called.

"OK! I'm coming!" Lia replied. She put her hairbrush down, turned the music off, and picked up her book bag. "Another day, another seven hours of school full of annoying teenage boys," she said to herself.

Chapter 1

All of the boys in her class were very annoying, especially Jaden. He would always make fun of her hair and pelt spitballs at her. Lia wouldn't really consider this bullying because it didn't really bother her and she would always find a creative and subtle way to get him back. But it was still really annoying to her.

"Lia!" her mom called again.

"I'm coming!" Lia replied. Lia was about to leave when she heard her kitten, Snowball, meow behind her. She turned around and saw her kitten sitting on her bed. Snowball had fluffy, long white fur. "Snowball, I can't play now. I have to go to school," Lia said to her kitten.

Snowball meowed again and put her paw on a notebook on top of her bed. "Oh. My notebook. I can't believe I almost forgot this. Thanks, Snowball. You're a lifesaver." Lia took the notebook from under her kitten's paw and put it in her book bag. "Bye, Snowball. See you after school," Lia said as she left her bedroom.

***

At Alex's house, Alex was sitting at the table eating breakfast with his mom and dad. However, instead of eating breakfast, he was playing a video game on his phone. "Yes! I finally beat level 20!" Alex took a screenshot of the game on his phone and started posting it on social media.

"Son, do you think you can take a break from your phone so you can finish your breakfast?" his dad asked him.

Alex looked at the almost-soggy bowl of cereal in front of him. He put his phone down on the table. "Sorry, dad. I just had to post it before someone else did."

"You kids today with your cell phones and social media. You know, when your father and I were kids, we didn't have the Internet," Alex's mom said.

"Yeah, I know. You guys had messenger pigeons to text each other," Alex said jokingly. Alex's dad ruffled up Alex's hair.

"Now finish your breakfast so you can get to school on time," his mom said. Alex's mom went into the kitchen. His dad continued reading the newspaper in his hands. Alex took a few spoonfuls of his cereal.

When he knew both his parents weren't looking, he grabbed his phone and typed a caption over the picture he was about to post. *Another day, another seven hours of school being awesome.* His phone chimed. It was a text message from one of the girls at school. "And also getting harassed by all the girls at school," he added. Alex put his phone in his back pocket.

Alex was very popular among the girls at his school. You'd think he'd like all the attention, but sometimes it got a little annoying. Some girls who choose to keep their distance but swoon over him from afar slip, like, a million notes into his locker per day. Another group of girls standby waving, giggling and twirling their hair. A few even managed to get his number somehow, like the girl who texted him a few minutes ago. And then there are the really bold type who come up and ask him a ton of ridiculous questions.

"What shampoo do you use? Your hair smells so good."

"Do you have a dog? If you don't have one, you can totally have mine."

"Are you allergic to nuts? If you are, then I am, too."

Alex had to go through stuff like this every single day at school. But he managed to get through it. "Bye, Mom. Bye, Dad. See you after school." Alex got up and headed for the door with his book bag. He picked up his skateboard and his helmet and left for school.

2

Partners?

The school bell rang and everyone rushed to class. The students were sitting in science class listening to the teacher, Mrs. C. She allowed the students to call her that because her last name seemed too long and complicated for them to remember. Mrs. C was talking about an upcoming project.

Many of the kids weren't paying attention. One boy was trying to balance a pencil on his nose, and one girl was doodling in her notebook. Julie was one of the few kids who was paying attention, but the way she was twirling her hair made her look like she wasn't.

Unlike most kids in her class, Julie kind of liked science. It was interesting to her because Justin did science experiments at home all the time. Julie listened to Mrs. C explain the project.

Mrs. C said, "I want you to pick a natural resource, find that natural resource in your local community, and write a report about it." She then stated that she posted a list of groups for the project in the back of the classroom. Everyone, except for Julie, ran to the back of the classroom to find out who was in their group.

Mrs. C noticed Julie sitting by herself. She walked over to Julie. Julie smiled when she saw her come over. Mrs. C was the only person Julie usually talked to at school. She couldn't really consider Mrs. C her "friend" because she's an adult and also her teacher, but she was always happy to have someone to talk to.

"Why didn't you go to the back of the room with the others? Don't you want to see who your partners are?" Mrs. C asked.

"I don't really care who my partners are. I know they'll just do the project themselves and exclude me, like they always do," Julie said.

"Aw, don't talk like that. Maybe it'll be different

this time," Mrs. C said. Julie shrugged. "I made this project a group project so people could make new friends, especially you, missy. Don't worry. You'll thank me later." Mrs. C walked away. She was about to sit back at her desk, but then Alex called her.

Mrs. C walked over to Alex. "Hi, I think you made a mistake here," Alex said, pointing at the list. He saw that he was assigned to a group with Lia and Julie.

"How so?" Mrs. C asked.

"You partnered me up with two girls," Alex explained.

"And?" Mrs. C asked.

"You know how the girls get around me," Alex said.

"Not these two. Trust me. You'll be fine," Mrs. C patted Alex's shoulder and walked away.

***

Lia became upset when she saw the board. "Why do I have to be in a group with a boy and that shy girl? I wanted to be partnered with you guys," Lia said to her two friends, Toni and Sneha.

"At least you get to be partners with Alex,"

Sneha said.

"Yeah. He's so dreamy," Toni chimed in, blushing.

"I don't know what you two see in him. He's just a boy."

Toni and Sneha gasped. "Alex isn't 'just a boy.' He's *the perfect* boy," Sneha said.

"Yeah. He can ride a skateboard, he has perfect hair, and he's super cute!" Toni added. The two of them started giggling. Lia rolled her eyes.

"Whatever. Who'd you two get assigned with?" Lia asked. Toni looked at the list.

"Aw man! We got partnered with Jaden," Toni complained.

"Ugh! Really? He's so obnoxious," Sneha whined.

"Well, good luck," Lia told both of them.

"Thanks, Lia," Toni said.

"Oh, and have fun with Alex," Sneha said following Toni towards their seats.

"Yeah right," Lia mumbled as she looked at the list again. She marched over to her seat and sat down.

Chapter 2

She was not happy.

Lia turned around and saw Julie in the desk behind her. "Hey," she said without any enthusiasm. Julie just looked up, waved, and gave half of a smile. Lia said, "I like your shoes." Julie looked at her boots, slid them under her desk, and didn't say anything.

Alex walked over to Julie and Lia and asked, "You two are in my group, right?"

"Yeah," Lia responded.

"So what do you want to do the project on?" Alex asked.

"We can do it on plants or something like that," Lia suggested.

"But plants can be poisonous, and you don't know where they've been," Alex responded.

"But plants don't move."

"Then how do they grow?"

"That's not what I—" Lia sighed. "Whatever. How about bugs?"

"Same thing. Some are venomous, and we don't know where they've been."

"But—" They started to argue back and forth.

After two minutes of arguing, Julie couldn't take it anymore. "I have a suggestion," she butted in. Lia and Alex both said "What?" in unison.

"Wait, you can talk?" Lia said surprised.

"Of course I can talk. I just choose not to," Julie answered.

"Well, what's your suggestion?" Alex asked.

"We can look for rocks! They aren't poisonous, and they don't move," Julie said.

"That's actually a really good suggestion," Alex said.

Julie smiled. No one ever took her suggestions in group projects before.

"Yeah. You should talk more often shy girl," Lia said.

Julie's smile fell when she heard her demeaning nickname. Lia covered her mouth when she realized what she'd just said. "OMG. I'm so sorry. I didn't mean to..."

"No. It's fine. I'm used to it." The bell rang. Julie collected her things and put them in her back pack. "You two have fun working on the project without me."

Chapter 2

She grabbed her bag, put her hoodie on her head, and left the room.

3

Weird Glowing Blue Rocks

Lia felt bad about what happened earlier with Julie and wanted to apologize. She didn't mean to call her shy girl. It just slipped out. During recess, Lia found Julie in the playground sitting on a swing. "Hey," Lia said as she sat down on the swing next to her. Julie acknowledged Lia with a nod. "I'm sorry about what I said earlier." Lia pushed herself back and forth on the swing.

"Lia, I told you I'm used to it. I really don't care."

"But I still feel bad that I—" Lia stopped swinging. "How do you know my name?" Science was one of the few classes the two of them had together. Lia knew Julie didn't walk over to look at the list during class so there was no way she could've known what her name was.

"You'd be surprised how much you can learn when you don't talk to people."

"Well, I'm still apologizing whether you want me to or not. And Alex and I think you should be included in our group project."

"Why? I'll just be a burden."

"No you won't. Without you, we wouldn't even know what to base our project on in the first place. I know you're smart. We need you for this project."

Julie looked at the ground. "I don't know," she murmured.

"Please," Lia begged her.

Julie shifted her eyes from the ground to Lia and back again. Lia was fluttering her eyes making herself very convincing and innocent looking. Julie sighed. "Alright. I'm back in."

"Yes!" Lia stood up. "Come on. Alex is waiting for us by that spot with all the rocks around it."

Julie knew the place she was talking about. That was one of the places she hid when she was trying to stay away from Crystie. A place to go so no one would see her crying.

"Hey. You ok?" Lia asked Julie, noticing she wasn't following her and was staring at the ground again.

"Yeah. Yeah. I'm fine. Let's go." Julie stood up and followed Lia even though she knew exactly where they were going.

The two of them found Alex leaning against a tree playing a game on his phone. "You know, you could've started without us," Lia said.

Alex paused his game and looked up from his phone. "Finally! You girls take forever."

Lia rolled her eyes. "I only took long because I was trying to make our friend feel better." Lia gave Julie a friendly punch on the arm and went over to an area with rocks around it. She got on her hands and knees and started searching for rocks. Alex put his phone in his back pocket and joined her. Julie stayed standing where she was, still in shock from hearing the word friend.

Julie didn't know if Lia said it just to be nice or if she really meant it. Julie really hoped she meant it. It would be really nice if she could have some friends for a change. It was definitely better than being alone.

"Hey, dude. You coming?" Alex called to Julie who was staring at the ground again. Julie got on her knees next to Lia and started looking for rocks with the two of them.

As the three of them searched for any rocks that looked interesting in any way, they all put them in their own piles. Alex looked at Lia's and Julie's piles and said, "Ha! I have more rocks than both of you." Lia became a bit annoyed and started to quickly gather more rocks. Eventually, they had all collected so many rocks that there was only dirt left on the ground.

Suddenly, they all noticed something blue and glowing in the ground, so they started to dig in the dirt with their hands. They found three small, glowing, dark-blue rocks. "Uh…why are those rocks glowing?" Julie asked.

"I don't know," Lia said. They tried to pick

them up, but the rocks shocked them before they could. The shock from the rocks wasn't like a normal shock from a door knob; it was about three times as painful as that.

"Ouch!" Alex screamed. "Did anyone else feel a surge of energy go through their bodies?" Alex asked. Julie and Lia both nodded.

"And look! The rocks aren't glowing anymore," Julie said. Lia and Alex both looked at the rocks and realized Julie was right. The rocks were no longer glowing.

"OK. This is just too weird," Alex said.

Being the brave girl that she was, Lia closed her eyes and slowly touched one of the blue rocks. Surprisingly, it didn't shock her this time. Lia picked the rock up. Lia said, "Hey guys! Pick them up again. They won't shock you."

Julie and Alex picked up the rocks. Then they placed the three rocks in their own pouch, separate from the normal ones so they wouldn't lose them. Lia took the bag of normal rocks home with her while Julie took the three blue rocks home.

Chapter 3

The next morning, Lia woke up and went over to the mirror to fix her hair. When she looked into the mirror, she didn't see her reflection. She jumped back, which caused her hairbrush to fall on the floor. After she picked up the brush, she looked in the mirror again. This time, she saw her reflection. *That was weird*, Lia thought. Lia knew she had to tell Julie and Alex about what happened.

On this same morning, Julie was at home eating breakfast with Justin. Justin was reading a book about psychics. When Julie stretched her arm out to get her glass of juice, the glass moved before she could touch it. She looked at Justin to see if he did something to make the glass move, but he was quietly reading his book.

Julie tried to pick up the glass again, but it fell off of the table. Justin looked up, startled by the noise, and then looked at the broken glass on the floor. "You know you have to clean that up, right?" Justin said.

4

Superpowers!

Julie maneuvered her way through the crowds of students in the hallway trying to get to her locker. She texted Lia and Alex to meet her there to talk about what happened to her this morning. The three of them exchanged numbers the day before so they could talk about the project outside of school.

Julie was standing by her locker waiting for her friends to get there when she heard someone behind her say, "Hey, look. It's shy girl." The brunette girl and her blonde friend walked by Julie and laughed.

"She's such a dweeb," the blonde girl whispered loudly to her friend.

Julie cringed and took her hand out of her

pocket to open her locker. When she moved her hand, Julie accidentally made the blonde girl's smoothie spill all over her friend's shirt and some of her hair.

"Tiffany, look what you did to me! You're such a klutz." The brunette girl stormed off trying to wipe the smoothie off of her shirt. The blonde girl followed her.

Julie laughed to herself a little. If only she could have done that everytime someone picked on her. Julie saw Lia walking toward her. "Hey, I'm glad you came. Something weird happened to me this morning."

"Me too! I looked in the mirror, and I didn't see myself!" Lia said.

"That's weird. At breakfast, I tried to pick up my glass of juice, and it moved away from me!" Julie said.

"Guys," Alex said as he walked over. "Look what I did to my alarm clock this morning." Alex took a burnt alarm clock out of his bag.

"How did this happen?" Lia asked as she took the alarm clock from him. Alex explained that his alarm clock went off, and when he went to turn it off, electricity came from his hand and set the alarm clock on fire. He managed to put the fire out after it happened.

Lia and Julie were baffled. They also told Alex about what happened to them.

"Maybe it had something to do with those blue rocks we found yesterday," Julie said. Julie took the bag of rocks from the day before out of her book bag.

"You brought the rocks to school?" Alex asked. "I left them in my book bag yesterday," Julie said. Lia suggested that they tell someone what was going on.

"No!" Alex said. "On television shows about superheroes, they never tell anyone their secrets!"

"There's also at least one person who knows. Do you ever read comic books?" Lia said.

"Come on, who reads comic books anymore? Those are for nerds," Alex said.

"Oh, so you're calling me a nerd now?" Lia said. They kept arguing back and forth. Again.

"Guys!" Julie interfered.

"What!" Alex and Lia shouted at the same time.

"I know someone who we can talk to about this," Julie answered.

"Who?" Lia asked.

"My little brother, Justin."

Chapter 4

Alex and Lia both started to laugh. Julie crossed her arms and waited for them to stop laughing. Lia looked at Julie and realized that Julie wasn't joking. "Oh, you're serious?" Lia asked.

"Yeah! Justin has an A+ grade average, he skipped three grades in school, and he's super smart. He's also really good at keeping secrets," Julie said.

"OK. But if he skipped three grades, then why doesn't he go to school here?" Alex asked.

"He goes to this preparatory school for kids like him. So can we tell him?" Julie asked. Alex and Lia both agreed that it was OK to tell Justin about what was going on.

5

Julie's Little Brother

Julie invited Lia and Alex over to her house so that they could talk to Justin. "I told my mom that I'm coming over to your house," Lia said.

"Me too," added Alex as he hung up from speaking to his mom.

"OK. Let's go to my house," said Julie.

After school, Lia and Alex walked home with Julie. "I like your house," Alex said. Julie did not respond. Julie had a really big house with a small garden in the front. There were also some stones scattered around small trees in the front yard. They walked into the house.

"Hi, Mom," Julie said.

Chapter 5

"Hi, sweetie," her mom said without looking up. She was very busy with work.

"We're just going to talk to Justin for a little while."

"We?" Julie's mom asked while looking up. "Oh my goodness, you made some friends," she said as she walked up to Lia and Alex and hugged them. Alex and Lia looked at Julie with confused looks on their faces. Her mom then let go of Alex and Lia.

"I need to get a picture of this on my phone. I don't know how to do that on my phone. Oh my, where are my manners? Julie, aren't you going to introduce me to your friends?" Julie's mom said.

"Mom, this is Lia and Alex. Lia and Alex, this is my mom," Julie said.

"Hi, Julie's mom," Lia and Alex both said waving.

"Oh please, call me Mrs. Peters or Mrs. Jennifer. You know what, call me whatever you want. You are Julie's friends after all," Julie's mom said.

"Mom," Julie said, getting a little embarrassed.

"I know, I'm embarrassing you in front of your

friends. This is all kind of new to me because Julie's never invited anyone over before," she said to Lia and Alex.

"Mom, listen. Lia and Alex and I are working on a science project and we need to talk to Justin about something," Julie told her.

"OK. Well, before you go, let me get your father. I want him to meet you two," Julie's mom said. She started walking out of the room. "Richard, honey, get in here!" she said.

"Let's go upstairs before she comes back," Julie whispered to Lia and Alex. They all started going upstairs.

"What was that all about?" Alex asked Julie.

"You two are the first people I've ever invited to my house. My mom's just making a big deal out of it," Julie explained.

When they reached Justin's room, Julie knocked on the door. "Hey, can I come in?" she asked.

"Yeah," Justin said. When they went inside of Justin's room, they saw books everywhere. There were books on the floor, on his bed, and on his night stand. There was also a small model of the solar system hanging from the ceiling, a Newton's cradle model on his desk, and a bunch of other science stuff around the room. Justin was doing homework on the computer.

"Can I talk to you about something?" Julie asked. "It's very important," she explained.

"OK. But make it quick because I have a lot of homework to do." He finally looked up and saw Alex and Lia standing there. "Who are they?" he asked.

"This is Lia and Alex. We're working on a science project together. That's kind of what I need to talk to you about. We found these weird, glowing blue rocks and then strange things happened to each of us the following morning. My juice moved away from me, Lia couldn't see herself in the mirror, and Alex fried his alarm clock."

Justin looked stunned for a moment. "Wow! Even I don't know the answer to that...yet. But if I analyze the rocks that you guys found, I might get an answer. I can't explain why this happened to you guys. But I do know that Lia has invisibility, Alex can emit electricity and you have telekinesis, which is the ability to move stuff with your mind." Julie looked at her hands in disbelief.

Justin continued talking. "Now, I know that this sounds super cool, but try not to use your powers because you don't know what damage you may cause with them." Lia and Alex looked at Justin and were a little upset.

"Oh, come on," Alex said. "You just told us that we have super cool powers and we can't even use them?"

"Yes, that is what I said. And you should take my advice," Justin said.

"But…" Lia started to complain.

"Come on guys, stop complaining. My brother's right. We shouldn't use our powers," Julie said.

Julie took Lia and Alex into her room and closed the door. Julie threw her book bag onto her bed. "Let's use our powers!" she said excitedly. Julie started to try to move a book on her desk in the middle of the room.

"Wait," Lia said. "I thought you just told us not to use our powers."

"I know," she said, while still trying to move the

book.

"I agree with you guys. I just didn't want to make a big fuss about it. Plus, I never take my brother's advice. So, what are you guys standing there for? Let's use our superpowers!" Lia and Alex looked at each other. Then they both became excited as well and smiled. None of them noticed, but while they were practicing, the rocks in the pouch, which were in Julie's backpack, started to glow.

6

Practice Makes Perfect

Julie, Alex, and Lia were practicing their powers. Julie finally managed to pick up the book. All she had to do was focus and make her hands tense to activate her telekinesis.

Lia figured out how to turn invisible. It was kind of like pulling an imaginary zipper down in front of her. She turned invisible, walked over to Alex, and tapped him on the shoulder. This made Alex jump.

Julie and Alex heard Lia laughing. Then Lia turned visible again and was standing behind Alex, laughing.

"Ha ha! Very funny," Alex said sarcastically.

"It *was* funny!" Lia said while still laughing.

Alex figured out how to use his electricity powers. He just had to make his hand stiff, and electricity came out. He managed to fix a light bulb in Julie's room.

"Thanks for fixing that," Julie said. "It's been dead for months."

"You're welcome," Alex said with a smile.

Julie, Alex, and Lia practiced their powers for an hour.

"You know what?" Lia asked. "We should probably do our homework and go home."

"Yeah," Alex said. They did their homework and then their parents came to pick them up.

Julie went back into her room to pack her school books. Her mom came into the room.

"Did you have fun with your friends, honey?" her mom asked her.

"Yeah. I had a blast. Who knew working on a project could be so much fun?" Julie said.

"You know, I am so proud of you, Julie," her mom said.

"For what?" Julie asked her.

"For making new friends. You haven't been able to do that for years," her mom answered.

"I know. I was pretty amazed too," Julie said.

"First, you make new friends. Soon, you'll be going to high school. Aw. My little girl's growing up so fast," her mom said.

"Don't worry. I won't be going anywhere soon." Julie and her mom both hugged.

"If you need me, I'll be in my room, OK?" Julie's mom said.

"OK," Julie said. Her mom left the room.

"Julie," she heard her brother call.

"Coming," she said in response. Julie walked into her brother's room. "You called me?" she asked.

Justin closed his bedroom door so that their parents would not hear their conversation. He had an upset look on his face. "I thought I told you not to use your powers," he said.

"How did you know that we were using our powers?" Julie asked.

"The walls aren't as thick as you think they are. I specifically told you not to use your powers. You don't know how dangerous they are," he said.

"You're just overreacting."

"No, I'm not," Justin said.

Julie crossed her arms. "Ugh! Why do you always act so stubborn?" Julie asked.

"I'm not being stubborn. I'm being headstrong," Justin argued.

"But come on," she said. "What would you do if you had superpowers one day? Like, super smarts?" Julie asked.

"Duh! Have you met me? I already have super smarts," Justin said. Julie knew he didn't actually have super smarts. But ever since he was little he always said he did.

"But look what I can do," Julie said.

Julie looked at Justin's messy room. Using her telekinesis, she picked up his shirt, opened the drawer, put the shirt in the drawer, and closed the drawer. She looked at Justin, but he was still unsatisfied.

Julie scanned the room and found an empty laundry basket by his bed. She then used her powers to lift up all the clothes one by one, fold them, and put them into the laundry basket. By the time she had finished, Justin's room was practically spotless. Now, Justin was satisfied. "See," Julie said with a smile.

"OK. OK. You have a point," Justin said.

"Now can I use my powers?"

"Sure, just not in public and only use them when you are with me, Alex, and Lia. Deal?"

"Deal." Justin held his hand out, but Julie hugged him instead.

"Ugh. You know I hate hugging," Justin said, smiling.

"I know," Julie said. Julie hugged him tighter. Julie let her brother go.

"Julie?" Justin asked.

"Yeah?" Julie asked.

"Thank you for cleaning my room," Justin said.

"You're welcome," Julie said back, and left the room with a smile.

7

Powers Gone Crazy

Julie, Lia, and Alex were in science class watching another group finish presenting its project. Mrs. C stood up from her desk. "Great job, you three. Lia, Julie, Alex, you're up."

Lia and Alex stood up and walked towards the front of the class. Julie dug through her folder and pulled out the paper she wrote for the project. Julie walked over to the teacher's desk and gave it to her. She then joined Lia and Alex at the front of the class.

For the project, they did not use the blue rocks they found because they did not want to lose them. Justin was studying them at home. They used a white stone, black shiny pebbles, and a dirty brown rock.

Lia and Alex were talking while Julie displayed the rocks because she was too shy to talk. Julie started to pick up one of the rocks, and it started shaking! Luckily, no one noticed. *Was that me?* she thought.

Julie tried picking up the rock again, but this time it flew off the table and across the room. Julie got down on the floor to look for the rock. She pulled on Lia's skirt, which made Lia go down on her knees. All the boys started laughing at Lia. "Shut up," Lia said back to them. All of the girls were staring at Alex while he kept talking.

"What is it?" Lia asked. "I think I moved the rock with my powers, and not on purpose," Julie said.

"Well what do you want me to do about it?" Lia asked.

"Uh…Lia?" Julie asked shaking a little.

"What is it *now*?" Lia asked.

"Your hair…" Julie pointed at one of Lia's ponytails. Lia looked at her hair. It started to disappear. "I think it's turning invisible," Julie said.

"We need to go somewhere private," Lia said.

Chapter 7

"We can go to the bathroom," Julie suggested. Lia put her invisible hair behind her shirt so no one else would see. Julie found the rock and put it back on the table. The teacher let them go to the bathroom. Alex stood there nervously as the girls in class stared at him, blushing.

They both quickly walked to the bathroom. "Science is last period so we can go to my house after school," Julie said.

"OK. What should we do in the meantime?" Lia asked.

"I guess we could stay in here. I used to do it all the time when…" Julie stopped.

She was thinking about how Crystie would bully her and she would hide in the stall to avoid her. "You're nothing, Julie Peters. Nothing at all. You're just a worthless, shy little girl. And that's all you'll ever be," Crystie would say. Her taunting echoed in Julie's head.

"When what?" Lia asked.

Julie snapped out of her thoughts. "Nothing," Julie said quickly. "Let's just stay in here until the end of the day."

"How do you think Alex is doing?" Lia asked. Julie shrugged.

Back in science class, Alex finished the presentation. He started picking up the rocks and dropped one of them on the teacher's desk. As he picked it up, his hand touched the stapler, and a little bit of electricity came out of his hands.

OK, he thought. *This is just my imagination. I did not just shock the stapler.* He walked over to his desk and started to pick up his things. He picked up his pencil, and he shocked the little metal part of it. *I need to talk to Lia and Julie*, he thought.

Alex opened the door with his elbow and walked toward the girls' bathroom. He knew that he could not go in, so he waited by the door. He tried to take his phone out to text Lia and Julie, but he shocked his phone. "Ugh! I am so tired of this," he said.

Alex had no choice but to go into the boys' bathroom, take his pants off, and shake his phone out. He bent down and texted Julie and Lia while his phone was still on the ground so that he wouldn't shock it.

Julie and Lia came out of the bathroom. Alex

was standing by the door. "What is it?" Julie asked.

"My powers are going crazy. I keep shocking everything that I touch that is made of metal," Alex said.

"Our powers are going crazy too!" Julie said.

"Wait, how did you text us? Your phone is made of metal," Lia said.

Alex glanced toward the bathroom, then he looked back at the girls. "You don't want to know," he said.

"During the presentation, I moved the rocks with my powers, and it was not on purpose," Julie said.

"And look at my hair!" Lia said. Lia took her hair out of her shirt. It was getting worse. It looked like she had one short ponytail and one long one.

Alex laughed. "What happened? Did you decide to give yourself a haircut?" Alex asked.

"No. It's invisible. See, feel." Lia started waving her hair in Alex's face.

"Stop it. That tickles," Alex said, laughing. "OK, seriously, stop it," Alex said, getting annoyed. Lia put her hair back in her shirt.

41

"So let's get our homework and go to my house so that we can talk to Justin," Julie said.

8

From Rocks to Rings

Julie, Lia, and Alex went to Julie's house after school. When they went into Julie's house, her mom hugged Lia and Alex again. "You guys came back!" she said while hugging them. Julie's mom stopped hugging them and took out her phone. "Good news. Thanks to Justin, I know how to take pictures with my phone now! Smile!" Julie's mom took a selfie with Julie and her friends in it.

"OK, so now how do I send it to you guys?" her mom asked them.

"Mom!" Julie said while feeling embarrassed.

"Sorry. I'm doing it again, aren't I? You guys go upstairs and have fun. I'm gonna try and figure out this phone myself." Julie, Lia, and Alex went upstairs and walked over to Justin's room.

Julie did not even knock on the door this time. She just opened the door and started to talk. "Hey, Justin," she said. "We need your help with something." She told him about everything that happened at school.

"I am so glad that all of those things happened to you guys," Justin said.

"You're glad that my hair is turning invisible?" Lia asked.

"No," Justin said. "I'm *glad* because my calculations were correct. I realized that you need those rocks to control your powers. After analyzing them, I realized that whatever energy was in the rocks went into your bodies when you touched them. That's how you got your powers. The rocks have to be near you in order for you to control your powers. It's like a radio to a radio tower. The closer the tower's signal is, the better the radio works. You can't carry the rocks around with you because there's a chance you could lose them, and it'd also be kind of weird. So I made you these."

Justin handed them three rings with the rocks

pressed into them. Lia and Julie put the rings on. Lia's hair went back to normal. Alex pushed his ring away. "No offense, but I am a boy and I don't wear jewelry," Alex said.

"Do you ever want to use your phone again?" Justin asked.

"Fine." Alex took the ring and put it on.

Alex, Julie, and Lia tested out their powers, and they were all back to normal. When they used their powers, the rings glowed. "Also, after hours and hours of research, I found out they're called kryodine rocks," Justin said.

"Hey, Justin?" Julie asked. "Where did you get the metal to make these rings?"

"I bought them from the craft store. They're made from old key chains, malleable metal wires, and I put it all together with my hot-glue gun," he said proudly. "Also, because you're wearing the rocks, you might get new powers. So don't freak out if weird stuff starts to happen." They all nodded.

"OK. So good luck, have fun, and goodbye." They all left the room and were admiring their new rings. Julie popped her head back in Justin's room and said, "Thank you."

"You're welcome," Justin said back.

"Oh, and please stop trying to teach mom how to use modern technology," Julie told him.

Justin laughed. "OK," he said. Lia and Alex packed their backpacks and went home.

9

Let's Make a Deal

Over the next few days, Lia, Julie, and Alex were worried about getting new powers because of what happened the last time, but nothing seemed to happen yet. Lia kept thinking that she would open the door, find out that she had fire powers, and accidentally burn down the entire school. But she knew that this was just in her head. They all decided to be more careful and try not to worry so much.

Julie was in a separate classroom from Lia and Alex. Julie was in math class. Her math teacher, Mrs. Cross, was teaching a lesson about percentages, and Julie was bored. Julie wanted to leave the classroom for a few minutes. Math wasn't Julie's best subject in school.

So she could leave, Julie raised her hand and asked, "Can I go to the bathroom?" Her teacher nodded and handed her a hall pass. Julie put the pass in her back pocket and walked out of the classroom.

Crystie was coincidentally in the hallway as well. Crystie had short red hair and always wore big hoop earrings. She was taller than most kids in the school, so she always made Julie feel small.

"Well, well, well. If it isn't shy girl," Crystie said. Julie looked at the floor.

"Actually, my name is..." Julie started to say, but Crystie cut her off.

"I don't care what your name is," Crystie said.

"Can I just go to the bathroom?" Julie asked.

"Why do you want to go to the bathroom? Are you afraid the kids are gonna pick on you?" Crystie teased.

"Can you please just leave me alone?" Julie asked, becoming frustrated.

Julie's hands were becoming tense. Her telekinesis becomes activated when her hands become tense. Neither of them noticed, but Julie was slowly opening up a locker in the hallway. "Aw, the shy girl wants to be alone. Are you gonna cry?" Crystie teased again.

Julie became angry at this point. "Will you just stop it?" Julie yelled. She balled her hands into fists and then the locker slammed shut. Julie realized what happened and immediately relaxed her hands.

Crystie turned around and looked at the lockers. "Did you see that?" Crystie asked.

"See what?" Julie asked nervously. She hid her ring behind her back in case it was glowing. She didn't want Crystie to see it.

"The locker," Crystie said while still looking at it. Julie ran down the hallway and turned a corner. She hid behind a bunch of book bags that were in the hallway.

I wish she would just go away, Julie thought. She peeked into the hallway to see if Crystie was nearby. She heard her coming down the hallway, so she went back behind the book bags. Crystie was in the hallway now.

"I know you're back there. There's no use in hiding," Crystie said. Julie slowly got up from behind the book bags and tried not to make eye contact with Crystie. "While you were hiding back there like a wimp, I found out your secret," Crystie said.

Julie looked at Crystie and was a little worried. *Did she find out about my powers?* she thought. Crystie held up a small picture of Alex. There was a heart around his face. Julie walked over and snatched the picture from her.

"Where did you get this?" Julie asked.

"From your locker," Crystie said.

"Well, how did you know it was mine? It could've been anyone's," Julie said.

"Then why was it in your locker?" Crystie asked her.

"Well, what if I was holding it for a friend?" Julie asked.

"Oh please. Like *you* have friends." Julie wanted to tell Crystie about Lia and Alex, but she didn't want her to start bothering them too.

"OK. It's mine. What are you gonna do now?"

Julie asked.

"I'm gonna tell Alex that you like him," Crystie said. She snatched the picture from Julie's hand and started to walk away.

No! If she tells Alex I like him, she'll ruin everything, Julie thought. Julie wished she could stop her so badly. But she couldn't do anything. She was completely helpless. Suddenly her stomach started feeling queasy. At first she thought it was just the nerves, but she soon realized it was something more than that because her ring was glowing on her finger.

It all happened so fast, Julie couldn't process exactly what happened to her. All she knew was that her vision got blurry, then went back to normal, and she was suddenly standing somewhere else. She teleported. Then she realized she was standing right in front of Crystie.

"How... how did you do that?" Crystie asked, shaking a little. *Oh no*, Julie thought. The first thing that popped into Julie's head was to lie. But with Crystie standing there and staring at her waiting for her to say something, she couldn't come up with one. She had no choice but to tell the truth.

"I have superpowers," Julie said. When Julie looked down, she noticed Crystie dropped the picture of Alex from her locker on the floor. Crystie looked down and noticed it too. Julie stepped on it and dragged it towards her before Crystie could get it. "Please don't tell anyone," she added as she picked up the picture and put it safe and sound in her pocket.

"And what makes you think I'll do that?" Crystie asked, a bit more relaxed now. She had a point. The two of them weren't friends. They were the opposite of friends in fact. But she didn't want Crystie to run off and tell everyone in the whole school about her powers. That would be bad. Julie had to say something. Anything.

"If you keep my secret, I'll do anything you want," Julie blurted out. Anything but that. She regretted saying it as soon as it came out of her mouth. A smile came across Crystie's face. That was a bad sign.

"Anything I want, eh?" Crystie thought for a moment. "OK, you have to do anything I say. No

Chapter 9

exceptions," she said. Julie started to fiddle with her ring. She tends to do that when she is nervous. She usually does it with the string of her hoodie, but her ring felt more comforting.

"Fine, I'll do it. You promise you won't tell anyone about any of this?" Julie asked.

"As long as you do anything I say. Do we have a deal?" Crystie asked while she waited for Julie to shake her hand. *I know I shouldn't trust her, but I'm desperate*, Julie thought.

"Deal," Julie said. They both shook on it. Then they both walked back to class pretending nothing ever happened.

10

Keep-Away

While Julie was in math class, Lia and Alex were in history class. Their teacher, Mr. Bret, was out sick, so they had a substitute teacher. The substitute teacher was not prepared, so she allowed the students to play outside. While outside, the students played a game called Keep-Away with a football.

Basically, in the game of Keep-Away there is a girls' team and a boys' team. The girls toss the football to the girls, and the boys toss the football to the boys. The goal is to try to stop the opposing team from getting the football. Lia thought it was pointless.

While everyone else played Keep-Away or as the class called it, "Boys versus Girls," Lia would sit and watch or do something totally different on her own. During the game, a boy named Jason bumped into Sneha. Sneha fell and broke her glasses so she had to sit out for the rest of the game.

Lia sat with Sneha. "I'm sad that my glasses broke," Sneha said.

"I wish that I could fix them," Lia said as she was taking them from Sneha.

"If I don't get these fixed by today, I'll have to wear my ugly old glasses. They make my eyes look huge," Sneha said. Lia started to fiddle around with Sneha's glasses. She found the broken piece and tried to fix it.

As Lia touched the glasses, the broken pieces stuck together. She realized that she froze the glasses back together. Sneha looked at her glasses, and her eyes widened. "You fixed them!" Sneha said in amazement. She took them from Lia and put them on. "Thanks," Sneha said. Sneha hugged Lia.

"You're welcome," Lia said after Sneha let her go. *I guess I just found out my new powers*, Lia thought as she looked at her hands.

Lia and Sneha were watching the game. Alex was playing with the other boys. The girls' team was winning. Toni and her other friend, Junie, were the only girls playing. All of the boys kept dropping the football, especially Alex. The ball kept slipping out of his hands.

The period ended and everyone started to head back to the building. While they were walking, Alex ran up to Lia. "Hey, can I talk to you for a second?" he said.

"Aw," her friends mouthed as they made heart shapes with their hands.

"Stop it," Lia mouthed back. She looked back at Alex.

"What do you want to talk to me about?" Lia asked.

"Remember I kept dropping the ball during the game?"

"Yeah. That was just sad," Lia said, shaking her head.

"Well, I wasn't dropping it. It went through my hands. I think I have new powers!"

"I have new powers too! I can freeze things!" Lia said.

Chapter 10

"Like Elsa?" Alex asked jokingly.

"Does Elsa have pink hair?" Lia asked him.

Alex laughed. "I wonder if Julie has new powers now."

When Lia and Alex reached the door, it was closed. They were locked out. "Aw man! How are we going to get in?" Lia complained.

"Hang on a sec. I got this," Alex said as he rolled up his sleeves. He looked around to see if anyone was looking. He then rubbed his hands together, stuck his arms through the door, and opened it.

"Ladies first," he said as he held the door open for Lia. Lia went inside and pushed the door closed. Alex was stuck outside again. Lia giggled and walked away. "Hey!" Alex yelled hitting the door. He tried opening the door, but it was locked. "Wait, what am I doing?" Alex walked right through the door and caught up with Lia.

11

I've Got a Secret

Lia and Alex found Julie in the hallway packing up her things. "Hey Julie," Lia said.

"We finally got new powers! I can go through things and Lia has ice powers," Alex said.

"Did you get any new powers, Julie?" Lia asked.

"Yeah! I can teleport! Watch!" Julie then teleported behind Alex and tapped him on the shoulder. He jumped and turned around to see Julie smiling.

"Why does this keep happening to me?" Alex murmured.

Julie looked over by the lockers and saw Crystie motioning for her to come over. "What are you looking at?" Lia asked.

Chapter 11

"Nothing. I just have to get something from my locker really quick," Julie said.

Julie then walked over to Crystie. "What do you need?" Julie asked.

"I need you to do my homework. I have a lot and don't feel like doing it," Crystie said as she placed a pile of books in Julie's hands.

"How am I supposed to do all of this and my homework?"

"I don't know. Figure it out yourself. I don't care as long as you get it all done." Crystie left and walked the other way. Julie sighed.

She retrieved the rest of her books from her locker and walked back over to where Lia and Alex were standing. Julie put her books and Crystie's books in her book bag. "That's a lot of books. Why do you have so much homework?" Alex asked Julie.

"A little extra homework never hurt anybody," Julie said, struggling to zipper her book bag. Julie tried to pull it up, but because of the extra books, the zippers on the book bag broke. "Really?" Julie said to herself.

***

"Are you OK?" Lia asked. "You seem a little down."

"I'm okay. I'm just tired from staying up late," Julie said. That was actually true. Julie couldn't sleep last night because Justin was busy working on a science experiment.

"Are you sure you're OK?" Lia asked again.

"Lia, can we go to the bathroom to talk in private?" Julie asked.

"OK," Lia said.

Julie started to pull Lia into the bathroom. After they were inside of the bathroom, Julie quickly peeked under the stalls to see if anyone else was in the bathroom. Julie wanted to tell Lia about the situation with Crystie, but she knew that she couldn't tell her. Not yet.

"I'm waiting," Lia said.

"I… uh…" Julie did not know what to tell her. "I like Alex," Julie blurted out.

"So?" Lia said.

"What do you mean?"

"Pretty much every girl in school likes him.

Well, every girl except for me."

"I know that. But the other girls like him because he is cute. I like him because of his personality."

Lia looked at Julie. "How long has this been going on?"

"Since I met him," Julie said.

"You know you will have to tell him eventually, right?" Lia asked.

"No way! I don't want him to think that I'm like all of the other girls."

"OK. I understand. I promise that I won't tell."

"Thanks." Julie and Lia left the bathroom, picked up their book bags, and walked home.

***

Julie lay in her bed wide awake. She levitated a pillow and made it spin over her head. Her ring was glowing, which made a blue light shine throughout the room.

Julie started to think about what happened with Crystie. She managed to complete both her and Crystie's homework with her brother's help. She was scared and knew that Crystie's requests were just going to get worse. Julie didn't want to think about it. So instead, she thought about all of the new things that had happened over the past few days.

She thought about her new friends and powers, getting an awesome ring, and spending more time with Justin. Julie also thought about how she was slowly overcoming her shyness. Thinking about all of these great things made her feel better. She used her powers and put her pillow down. Then Julie went to sleep.

12

What Is She Hiding?

During gym class, Alex was playing one-on-one basketball with Jason. Alex was losing because he couldn't focus. He felt that Julie was hiding something from him. "Can we take a quick break?" he asked.

"Sure. You definitely need one because you keep missing all of your shots," Jason said.

Alex and Jason sat on a nearby bench. "Hey, can I ask you for some advice?" asked Alex.

"Sure," Jason said. Alex didn't want Jason to find out about Julie because he thought that Jason would tell the other boys and they would all make fun of him.

"I have this friend. You don't know him. He

goes to a different school. I think that he's keeping secrets from me. What should I do?"

"Spy on him," Jason said.

"What?" Alex asked, confused.

"Spy on your friend. Don't stalk him at his house or anything like that. But try to listen in on his conversation and stuff. Trust me. It always works. Where do you think you would be if I didn't spy on you?"

"What?" Alex asked.

"Nothing," said Jason. Jason smiled.

"OK, we'll talk about that later. Spying on my friend *is* a good idea. And I know just the right person to help me," Alex said. He got up and started to look for Lia.

"What about our game?" Jason asked.

"There's always tomorrow," Alex said.

Alex found Lia bouncing a tennis ball near the school building. "Hey, Lia. Are you busy?"

"Nope. Just bouncing a tennis ball because I am bored out of my mind," Lia said.

"Good. I need your help with something. I think

that Julie is hiding—would you stop bouncing that ball?" Alex said, getting annoyed.

"Sorry," Lia said. She caught the ball in her hand. "What is it about Julie?"

"I think Julie is hiding something from me. Jason said that I should spy on her. And I need your invisibility to do it."

"I'm in," said Lia. "I think she is keeping something from the both of us. I want to figure out what she's hiding too."

"Great. Do you want to do this now or wait a little while?" Alex asked.

"I say wait. We should try to catch her in the act, instead of watching her all day." Lia and Alex agreed to spy on Julie the following day.

13

Help Me Break In, Weirdo

Julie was sleeping in her room when she heard a weird sound. It sounded like something was hitting her window. She got out of bed and walked over to the window. Someone was throwing things at it. Julie opened the window and saw Crystie throwing pebbles at her window in order to get her attention.

"What is it?" Julie loudly whispered.

"Come down here and I'll tell you," Crystie said. Julie teleported outside to where Crystie was standing. Crystie jumped. "I forgot that you can do that!"

While looking at her watch, Julie said, "What do

you need this late at night?" It was 11:30 p.m.

"I forgot to get a book that I need for school from the library, and I need you to break into the library to help me get it," Crystie said.

"No way! I am not breaking into the library. If we get caught, we might go to jail."

Crystie then said, "One, we won't get caught because you're helping me. And *two*, you must do whatever I tell you to do because of our deal, remember?"

"OK. I'll do it. But let me change my clothes first."

Julie teleported upstairs and changed into a shirt and a pair of jeans as fast as she could. Then she teleported back outside. "Hold my hand," Julie said.

"Ew, why?" Crystie asked.

"Just do it." Crystie then held Julie's hand. Julie teleported both of them to the library. They were both on the inside.

"It's kind of dark in here," Crystie said.

"How are you going to find your book in the dark?" Julie asked.

"I know. Use your ring light thingy," Crystie said.

"You mean this?" Julie said as she held her hand up and showed her ring.

"Yeah." Julie squinted in the dark and found a small book. She lifted it up with her powers and her ring started to glow.

"Can you make it a little brighter?" Crystie asked.

"No. This is all that I can do," Julie said. Crystie and Julie walked over to the adult section in the library.

"What kind of book do you need?" Julie asked.

"I need a book about rocks. But how will we find it without the librarian?" Crystie pointed at the empty desk.

"Easy. I just have to go onto the computer and find what you're looking for." Julie went over to the computer and turned it on. She put the book she had lifted down once the computer turned on. Then she started to type. Crystie just sat and watched. Crystie looked at Julie's ring.

"Hey, this is going to sound like a really weird

question, but why do you wear that ring?"

"It helps us to control our powers," Julie said while still looking at the computer.

"Wait, *us*?" Crystie asked.

Julie stopped typing. She looked up worried. She couldn't think of a lie fast enough. "Lia, Alex, and I all have superpowers," Julie said. *Why do I stink at keeping secrets?* Julie thought.

"Who's Lia?" Crystie asked.

"She's a friend of mine. Please don't tell them that you know. If you do, then they probably won't want to be my friend anymore. And they're the only friends that I have."

Crystie sighed. "This doesn't mean that we're friends or that I like you at all, but I feel sorry for you. So I won't say anything," Crystie said.

"Thank you. Now, let me finish finding your book so that we can get out of here," Julie said.

Julie went back to typing. After about one minute, Julie found the book options. She wrote down the possible choices and started to walk down the aisles to look for them. She then lifted the book back up so that her ring would start to glow again. Crystie followed Julie down the aisles.

Julie and Crystie eventually found the book. "Finally!" Julie said.

"Great! Now we can get out of here," Crystie said.

"We can't leave yet. I still have to check out your book with your library card," Julie said.

"Ugh! This is so much work," Crystie said.

"Don't complain. You're the one who forced me to come here. Now hurry up and give me your library card," Julie said.

"Actually, I left mine at home. So we have to use yours," Crystie said.

Julie took her library card out of her back pocket. "You are so lucky I always keep my library card in my back pocket."

Julie walked over to the main desk. She turned on the computer and started to type again. "How do you know how to do all of this stuff?" Crystie asked.

"My little brother taught me," Julie said as she was looking at the computer.

Chapter 13

"Is your little brother smarter than you?"

"Yeah. I know. Weird, right? He skipped, like, three grades. He always tries to teach me stuff that I don't need to learn, like how to make a clock or how to work the library's computer system. Speaking of which, can you scan this for me?" Julie handed Crystie her library card. Then Crystie scanned the card and gave it back to Julie.

"Yes! We're finally done! *Now* we can get out of here." Julie took Crystie's hand and teleported back to her house. "Take your book and go home. I don't want you to get in trouble." She gave Crystie her book. "Good luck. I'm going back to bed." She was about to teleport back into her bedroom, but then she stopped. She saw Crystie struggling to hold the book and ride her bike at the same time. Julie couldn't stand to see her like that.

Julie walked over to Crystie. "Hey, what's your address?" Julie asked.

"Ten Mulberry Lane. Why are you asking?" Crystie asked. Julie held Crystie's hand and teleported both of them along with Crystie's bike to her street.

"Hey, this is my street. Why'd you take me home?" Crystie asked.

"Because unlike you, I'm a nice person," Julie said.

Julie was about to teleport back to her house. "Wait," Crystie said.

"Do you want me to do something else for you?" Julie asked.

"No. I just wanted to say that I had fun tonight. You're not as lame as I thought you were," Crystie said.

"Oh. Well, thanks, I guess. See you tomorrow." Julie then teleported back home and into her bedroom.

As Julie changed back into her pajamas, she thought about what Crystie said. Was Crystie actually trying to be nice to her? Maybe because they were together more often, she was starting to warm up to her? Julie shook it off. *If she was warming up to me, she would've called off the deal,* she thought. Now in her pajamas, Julie went back under the covers and fell asleep.

14

Super Spies

Awesome Boy to Ponytails, what is your position?"
Alex said, talking into a small walkie-talkie.

"I'm right behind you," Lia said. She was
standing behind Alex. Alex jumped and turned around
to see Lia standing behind him. "Alex, what are you
doing?" Lia asked him.

"It's Awesome Boy. And where's your walkie-
talkie?" Alex asked her.

"Give me that." Lia snatched the walkie-talkie
from Alex and threw it behind her.

"Hey!" Alex cried.

"Just follow my lead and try to stay quiet," Lia
told him. Lia and Alex walked through the halls to see

if they could find Julie.

When Lia turned the corner, she saw Julie talking to someone. "I found Julie. She's talking to a girl with short red hair," Lia said.

Alex turned the corner and looked at the girl. Then he turned back to Lia. "That's just Crystie. She's in my math class," Alex informed her.

"But why would Julie be talking to her?" Lia asked.

"Let's listen in," Alex said. Lia and Alex held hands and soon they were both invisible.

"Being invisible is so weird," Alex said, looking at his hands that he couldn't see.

"You'll get used to it," Lia said.

They walked over to Julie and Crystie. Although they couldn't be seen, they still tried to stay quiet. "OK, so here's my to-do list," Crystie said to Julie. Crystie handed Julie a piece of paper filled with things that she needed Julie to do.

"Why don't you just do it yourself?" Julie asked.

"Because I don't feel like it," Crystie said.

"Besides, why do I have to keep reminding you? If you don't do whatever I say, then I'm going to tell everyone that you *and* your friends have superpowers."

"Shhh. OK. I'll do all of this stuff for you," Julie said.

"Great. Oh, by the way, I need it all done by tomorrow. 'Bye." Crystie skipped away to her next class, holding her books. Julie looked at the list. She gathered all of her things and walked away.

When Julie left, Lia turned herself and Alex visible again. They were both still holding hands. Alex and Lia both looked down and immediately let go of each other. "Let's never talk about that again," Lia said.

"Agreed," Alex said, wiping his hand on his pants.

"I can't believe Julie told that girl about our powers!" Lia said. "The only thing I don't understand is *why*," she said.

"I think we should talk to her about this," Alex said. "I mean, what if Crystie found out and threatened her?" he asked.

"You're right," Lia said. "We can talk about this

75

the next time we see her." They both got their books and went to class.

15

Wanna Come to a Sleepover?

A few periods later, it was lunchtime. Lia and Alex were in line getting their lunch. "So, how did you get so good at spying?" Alex asked Lia.

"Well, it's not the first time I've done it," Lia said. Alex got a little nervous because he didn't know if she ever spied on him before.

"What do you want to do about Julie?" Alex asked.

"We should try to talk to her during lunch," Lia said. "If she doesn't want to talk to us about it, I have a plan." Alex looked confused, but he went along with it.

The cafeteria was very crowded. They found

Julie sitting at a table by herself. They both walked over to where she was. Julie looked up and saw them coming over. Lia and Alex sat down across from Julie.

"What's up?" Julie asked. Lia and Alex looked at each other and then looked at Julie. "What's wrong?" Julie asked after seeing the expressions on their faces.

"Julie, we know about Crystie," Lia said. Julie froze.

"You do?" Julie asked, feeling worried. They both nodded. "Did Crystie tell you?" Julie asked.

"Actually, no, she didn't," Lia said.

"Then, how did you guys find out?" Julie asked.

"We—" Alex started to speak and was about to tell Julie that they spied on her but then Lia kicked Alex's leg under the table. "Ow!" Alex cried.

"We can talk about that later," Lia said with a smile on her face. She looked at Alex with an angry expression on her face. Then she looked back at Julie. "Julie, why did you tell her?" Lia asked.

Julie put her head in her hands. "I don't want to talk about it," she said. Then Julie's phone chimed. Julie looked at it. "Speaking of which, it's her," she said with a sad look on her face. "I'll be right back." Julie crawled under the table and teleported away.

"So, what's your plan?" Alex asked.

"You'll see," Lia said.

Julie teleported over to the vending machine where Crystie was standing. "What do you need now?" Julie asked her.

"This stupid machine took my stupid dollar so I need you to get my snack out for me," Crystie said.

"What snack are you getting?" Julie asked her.

"That one." Crystie pointed to a bag of chips in the machine.

Julie tried to grab the bag out of the machine with her powers, but instead, all of the snacks fell to the bottom of the machine. "Sorry," Julie said.

"*Sorry?* More like 'You're welcome.' I just got, like, twenty free bags of chips because of you!" Crystie said.

"Those weren't for free," Julie said.

"They will be as soon as you give me a dollar," Crystie said, holding her hand out.

Julie sighed and dug into her pocket. She pulled

out a five-dollar bill. "Can you break a five?" Julie asked.

"Nope," Crystie said as she snatched the money out of Julie's hand. Crystie put the five-dollar bill in her pocket.

"Hey, guys! Free snacks in the vending machine!" Crystie shouted to a group of girls sitting at a table. Apparently, she was sitting with them earlier. All the girls cheered and walked over to the vending machine. Most of them got on their knees to get the snacks from the bottom. The other girls stood behind them and waited for the other girls to leave.

One girl noticed Julie standing nearby the vending machine. "Get lost, shy girl," she said as she pushed Julie aside. Julie hated it when people called her "shy girl" to her face like that. Julie went behind a corner where no one could see her and teleported back under the table where Lia and Alex were sitting.

Julie then crawled out from under the table. "What happened?" Alex asked.

"I just had to get her a snack out of the vending machine and give her a dollar," Julie said. She lied. She didn't want to tell them the whole story.

"Hey, Julie?" Lia said. "It's Saturday tomorrow, and I was wondering if you wanted to sleep over at my house tonight?"

Julie perked up. "I would love that! It's just…"

"What?" Lia asked.

"I've never been to a sleepover before," Julie said, a little ashamed.

"Don't worry. I'll make sure you have a lot of fun."

"Thanks. I'll tell my mom." Julie walked away and started to dial her mom's number.

"Hey, Lia?" Alex said. "How is a sleepover going to make Julie talk?"

"You're a boy. You wouldn't understand. When I'm ready, I'll call you, and I will put you on the speaker phone so that you can listen in."

"Haven't we already done enough spying?"

"Last time. I promise."

16

Tell Me the Truth

Julie was at Lia's house for the sleepover. Julie walked into Lia's room. "Guess what my favorite color is?" Lia asked.

"Judging by your room, I'm guessing pink," Julie said. She looked around Lia's pretty pink bedroom. Julie felt something tickle her on her leg. She looked down and saw a kitten nuzzling up on her ankle. "Aw, your cat is so cute!" Julie said as she squatted down to pet it. Lia squatted down and started petting it with her.

"Thanks. Her name is Snowball. She's three years old," Lia said.

Chapter 16

"I wish I had a pet," Julie said.

"Well, be careful what you wish for. Snowball is a lot of work. You're lucky you have a little brother who you don't have to clean up after," Lia said. Julie laughed.

"That reminds me—I need to get her out of here because if she stays in my room too long, she pees. Come on, Snowball. Let's go," Lia said as she picked up her kitten and put her in the hallway. The kitten meowed and walked down the hallway. Lia walked back into her room. "OK, now that we got that out of the way, let's put on our pajamas and start having fun!"

Lia and Julie put on their pajamas. After that, they sat on Lia's bed trying to figure out what to do first. "We can watch a movie." Lia suggested.

"Movies are boring to me," Julie responded.

"We can draw."

"I'm not that good."

"We can braid each other's hair."

"I like my hair the way it is."

"Well, what do you want to do then?" Lia asked.

Julie thought for a moment and then snapped

her fingers. "We can play with our powers," she said.

"That sounds like fun. What should we do first?" Lia asked.

"Let me show you what I can do with a pillow," Julie said. She took a pillow from Lia's bed and lifted it in the air with her powers. Then she spun it around in the air and put it back on the bed.

"That's so cool! Hey, speaking of *cool*, do you like ice pops?" Lia asked her.

"Yeah," Julie said.

"I'll be right back," Lia said. A few minutes later, Lia came back with a box full of ice pops. "OK, what flavor do you want? I have grape, orange, cherry, you name it," Lia said. Julie looked in the box.

"Aw, they're melted," Julie said.

Lia looked in the box and saw melted ice pop liquid all over the inside of the box. "Don't worry. I got it," Lia said. Lia took one of the slightly melted ice pops out of the box. She used her ice powers to freeze the ice pop back to its original state.

Lia handed her the ice pop. "Nice!" Julie said, impressed.

Chapter 16

"Thanks. You should see what else I can do," Lia said as she took an ice pop out of the box. Eventually, Lia and Julie finished eating them.

"Hey, Lia?" Julie said.

"Yeah?" Lia responded.

"Thanks for giving me the best night ever," Julie said.

"You're welcome." They both hugged.

Lia's phone rang. It was Alex. They both stopped hugging. "Who's that?" Julie asked as she leaned over and tried to look at Lia's phone.

Lia took her phone and put it behind her back. She got up and started walking backward toward the door. "Oh, it's nobody. Just a friend of mine. I'll be right back." Lia left her room and went into the hallway. She answered the phone.

"Hey, Alex. What is it?" Lia asked.

"Are you ready to talk to Julie about Crystie yet?" Alex asked.

"Yeah. I was just about to call you. Are you ready?" Lia asked him.

"Yup. Hang on a second. I have to charge my

phone. I don't want it to die while I'm eavesdropping."
Lia heard electricity crackling over the phone. The
noise stopped.

"What was that?" Lia asked.

"I charged my phone with my powers."

"Oh. Well, stay on the phone. I'm about to talk
to Julie. Try to stay quiet."

Lia walked back into her room. "Hey, Julie.
Do you mind talking to me about something kind of
personal? About you?"

Julie looked confused. "Like what?" she asked.

"Do you think we can talk about Crystie?" Lia
asked nervously.

Julie froze. "No way! I told you that I don't
want to talk about it," Julie said.

"But we're best friends, and best friends do not
keep secrets from each other," Lia said.

"OK. I'll tell you."

"It all started in the sixth grade. It was my first
day at Princeton Middle School. I didn't know anyone
yet. Crystie was in my homeroom. Everyone in class
had to take a small quiz to see what we knew. I got

the highest grade out of everyone else. Crystie got the lowest grade. For some reason, she told everyone else that I cheated, and everyone believed her. I was really hurt when she did that. Ever since then, she was constantly picking on me. I was afraid that everyone else would treat me that way, so I never tried to make any friends. That is why I'm so shy. Eventually, nobody remembered my name, and everyone started calling me 'shy girl.'" Lia felt bad because before she met Julie, she always called her that, too.

"Then, about a few weeks ago, she found out that I had powers. The only way that she agreed to not tell anyone is if I agreed to do anything she wanted me to do. 'No exceptions,'" she said mockingly. "Then, when we snuck into the library, she—"

Lia cut Julie off. "You two snuck into the library?"

"Her demands are pretty high. Anyway, when *that* happened, Crystie found out that you and Alex also have powers. But she promised not to tell you guys that she knew because she surprisingly felt bad for me. The only reason I didn't tell you and Alex about all of this was because I was afraid you wouldn't want to be my friends anymore."

"I'm sorry, Julie. I didn't know she bullied you," Lia said.

"It's OK. I've never told this to anyone. Are we still friends?" Julie asked nervously.

"Of course we are! When Alex and I found out, I invited you to a sleepover. So you know I would never stop being your friend over something like that," Lia said.

"Thanks, Lia," Julie said. They both hugged again.

"So, how *did* you guys find out about Crystie?" Julie asked.

"Do I really have to tell you?" Lia asked.

"Best friends don't keep secrets from each other, remember? Those were your words," Julie said.

"OK. Keep in mind, this was all Alex's idea. We kind of spied on you with invisibility. We weren't stalking you or anything like that. We just watched you talk to Crystie about something. Are you cool about this?"

"Yeah. Just no more spying on me."

"I promise. No more spying."

"Great, Lia. Why did you have to tell her? What's the point of spying if you tell someone?" Alex said over the phone.

"Alex? Were you eavesdropping on us this entire time?" Julie asked.

Lia grabbed her phone and hung up. "OK. No more spying, starting now."

17

Jealous!

I don't think it's right that she's forcing you to do all of this," Alex said while looking at the extra books in Julie's hands.

"Actually, I feel like I deserve all of this. I told Crystie our secret, and I feel very guilty about it. But the more work she gives me, the less guilty I feel," Julie said.

"I still think it's wrong," Alex said.

"I agree with Alex," Lia said.

"We understand now, so you don't have to feel guilty anymore."

"Yeah," Alex said. "I think we should try to stop her."

Chapter 17

"I *don't* think we should try to stop her. She's my problem, not yours. So I should fix it." Julie noticed that Lia and Alex were looking at someone behind her. "What is it? She's right behind me, isn't she?"

"Yup," Crystie said.

Julie turned around. "So, I'm assuming your little friends know about me now," Crystie said.

"Yeah. What do you need now?" Julie asked.

"Actually, I'm here to talk to Alex. I already gave you stuff to do." Crystie then walked over to Alex.

"What do you want to talk to *me* about?" Alex asked.

"No hard feelings, but because you are friends with Julie, I don't like you anymore. I know. Doesn't sound like a big deal. Oh, and by the way, I also told your little guy friends that you're friends with Julie, too. Bye!" Crystie then skipped away. Alex looked past Lia and Julie and saw his friends laughing at him at the end of the hallway. He knew that's what would happen if they found out about Julie.

"I know I disliked her before, but now, I hate her," Alex said. Sparks of electricity started coming out of Alex's hands.

"Alex, calm down," Julie warned him. She realized his powers were acting up because he was getting mad like she had before.

Alex screamed and tried to run after Crystie, who was now at the other end of the hallway, but Julie stopped him. Julie grabbed him by his backpack with her telekinesis so he couldn't go anywhere. "Let me go!" Alex cried.

"Not until you calm down," Julie said.

"Julie, I know you want to fix this on your own, but no one should have to go through this by themselves," Lia said.

"Can you at least talk to her?" Alex asked, still struggling to get away. Julie didn't say anything. She just looked at her shoes.

"Hey, now that I think about it, I believe that Crystie is jealous of you," Lia said.

"No. That's impossible. No one could be jealous of me," Julie said.

"Just think about it. She bullied you because you got an A and she didn't," Lia told her.

"Still," Julie said. "Who would be jealous over that one little incident during all of this time? I think she picks on me for some other reason."

"Like what?" Lia asked.

"I don't know. But I know that she's not jealous of me."

"OK. If you say so," Lia said. "But when she admits it, I'm saying 'I told you so,'" Lia said.

"OK. I'm calm. You can let me go now," Alex said with his arms folded.

Julie stopped using her powers on Alex's backpack, and Alex fell on the floor. "Sorry," Julie said.

Lia laughed. "Again! Again!" she said, still laughing.

***

A couple of periods later, Alex was walking through the hallway and ran into his friends. They were still laughing at him for the whole Julie thing. "Hey, guys," Alex said to them.

"Dude, I cannot believe you're friends with 'shy girl'!" Jason said, laughing. The other boys started laughing with him. Alex didn't like the fact that they were laughing at Julie like that. He had to stand up for her.

"Her name is Julie," Alex said. His friends stopped laughing. "And Julie's my best friend. Sure, she doesn't talk to most people, and she may be a little socially awkward. But she's still the nicest, prettiest, most loyal friend anyone could ask for. So laugh all you want, but just know that she's a much better friend than any of you are."

Alex then walked away from his friends. Alex saw Julie watching him at the end of the hallway. "Thanks, Alex. That was really sweet," Julie said.

"You're welcome. I got your back, buddy." Alex kindly punched Julie in the arm and walked away. Julie smiled and watched him leave.

18

Busted!

During study hall, Julie was cleaning her locker. It was a mess. She wanted to straighten it up so that her books wouldn't fall out. She was the only one in the hallway. Crystie came out of the classroom and walked over to Julie.

"Hey, can you do my homework for me tonight?" Crystie asked as she handed her books to Julie. Julie did not look up and just continued to clean her locker. "Hey, I'm talking to you!" Crystie said loudly. "Are you going to do my homework or not?"

"Why do you bully me?" Julie finally asked.

"I'm not answering that."

"Why do you bully me?" she asked again.

"Can you just take my homework already?"

Crystie asked.

"I'm not doing anything for you until you answer my question," Julie said.

"Well, if you don't do what I say, I'm gonna tell your secret," Crystie said.

"OK," Julie said.

Crystie looked surprised that Julie wasn't freaking out. "I'm gonna tell," Crystie said.

"OK. Tell," Julie said. Crystie took her phone out.

All of a sudden, her phone flew out of her hand and started to float down the hallway. Crystie looked at Julie.

"Julie!" she cried. Julie put her hands in the air. "That's not me. But I think I know who it is," Julie said.

Lia became visible and was running down the hallway with Crystie's phone. Lia was laughing.

"It's your stupid little friend. Get back here with my phone, you weirdo!" Crystie said.

"You have to catch me first!" Lia said. Crystie started to run down the hallway after Lia. Julie followed.

Chapter 18

Crystie caught up with Lia, grabbed her arm, and snatched her phone out of Lia's hands. "Ha! Gotcha!" Crystie said as she took her phone back and let go of Lia's arm.

Then Alex came out of the wall and tripped Crystie. Crystie fell on the floor, and her phone flew into the air. Alex caught it. "Lia, go long!" Alex shouted. Lia ran and Alex tossed the phone to her. Lia caught it and continued running. Crystie got up and started chasing Lia again.

"Good job, Alex," Julie told him. They both high-fived.

"Thanks," Alex said back.

"Now you go back to class. Lia and I have got it from here," Julie said. Alex ran down the hallway into his homeroom. Julie followed Crystie and Lia down the hallway.

Lia went into the girl's bathroom. Crystie and Julie followed her inside. Crystie found Lia in a bathroom stall holding her phone over the toilet. "Take one more step and I'm dropping your phone in the toilet," Lia said.

"You wouldn't," Crystie said.

"Yes, she would," Julie said.

"You were in on this, weren't you?" Crystie asked Julie.

"Yup. The whole thing," Julie said.

"Now, if you want your precious phone back, answer my friend's question," Lia said.

"I don't want to. It's embarrassing," Crystie said.

"My arms are starting to get tired. I might as well just drop your phone in," Lia said. Lia started swinging the phone back and forth.

"Fine! I'll tell you," Crystie said. Lia stopped swinging the phone. Crystie then looked at Julie. "I'm jealous. There, I said it," Crystie said.

"I told you so," Lia told Julie.

"Shut up, *Lula*," Crystie said.

"It's Lia," Lia said.

"Whatever," Crystie said.

"Crystie, why would you be jealous of me?" Julie asked.

"Because you're smart, you're pretty, and you're

a very nice person. Plus, I'm pretty sure if you had made friends over the past two years, you'd probably be the most popular girl in school," Crystie told her.

"You really think so?" Julie asked.

"I know so," Crystie said. "I'm sorry I told everyone that you cheated on that stupid test in the sixth grade. I just got so mad that I got the lowest score. I felt that I had to blame someone, so I blamed you." Julie could not believe what she was hearing. Crystie was actually jealous of her. "You know what?" Crystie said. "The deal's off. You don't have to do my homework or anything else for me from now on."

"Really? Man, this day just keeps getting better and better."

"When I found out that you have powers and you like Alex, I became super jealous. I took advantage of your secrets, and I'm sorry for everything. Oh, that reminds me—here's your five dollars back." Crystie dug through her back pocket. She pulled out a five-dollar bill. Crystie handed it to Julie.

Julie pushed the money back toward Crystie. "You can keep it. You need it more than I do," Julie said.

"Thanks," Crystie said.

"You're welcome," Julie said.

"Now that I've apologized"—Crystie looked at Lia—"can I have my phone back now?" Crystie asked.

Lia sighed. "Fine." Lia tossed Crystie's phone to Julie. Julie caught it. Crystie tried to reach for it, but Julie held it back. "Now, before I give this back to you, do you promise not to tell anyone about our powers?" Julie asked.

"I promise," Crystie said.

"OK, here you go," Julie said.

Julie gave Crystie her phone. "Thanks," Crystie said. She put her phone in her pocket.

"You're welcome. I guess this sort of means we're friends now," Julie said.

"Yeah, I guess it does. Well, I'll see you around. Bye," Crystie said.

Crystie left the bathroom. "Wow. I knew she was jealous, but I wasn't expecting all that," Lia said.

"Me either," Julie agreed.

"Hey, what was that about?" Lia asked.

Chapter 18

"What was *what* about?" Julie asked, confused.

"When we discussed this earlier, I thought you said I would get to drop her phone in the toilet. Fun killer," Lia said as she crossed her arms.

Julie smiled and shook her head. "Can I drop *your* phone in the toilet?" Lia asked, hoping she'd say yes.

"No!"

19

The Dream

Julie was asleep in her bed. She opened her eyes and realized that she was not in her bed at all. There was grass all around her. She was lying on a stone path. *Where am I?* she thought. It sounded all echo-y. She stood up and turned around. She saw a building in the distance, but she couldn't see it that well. She walked up closer to it. It said "Extraordinary Academy" in big letters.

"Julie…" she heard someone call.

"Who said that?" she called back. She heard it again, but this time, it was louder. And it sounded like Justin's voice. Then Julie woke up.

Justin was sitting on her bed. "Julie! Get up!

Chapter 19

You're going to be late for school!"

Julie looked at her alarm clock. It was 7:30 a.m., and she was supposed to wake up at 7:00 a.m. "Oh my gosh!" she screamed. She quickly got up and started to get dressed.

"Hey. By the way, while you were sleeping, your ring was glowing. I didn't see you using your powers, so I was a bit worried."

Julie stopped and looked at her ring. "That's weird. I wasn't even using my powers. Although I had a really weird dream about some school."

"Tell me all about it," Justin said.

Julie put her sneakers on and went into the bathroom. "Why do you love it when weird things happen to me?" she asked as she brushed her hair.

"It's better than all of this math homework that I'm always doing."

Julie quickly brushed her teeth and ran downstairs. Justin followed her. "Hey, when you get to school, ask Lia and Alex if anything weird happened to them too, OK?" Justin asked.

"Of course I will. Come on, let me take you to

your bus stop. I'll tell you about my dream as much as I can on the way."

"Yay!" said Justin.

Julie grabbed two pieces of toast for the road. Justin and Julie grabbed their backpacks and walked out the door. "Bye, Mom," they both said. They both left and walked to Justin's bus stop. Julie talked about her dream the whole way there. "Well, that's everything I can remember," Julie said.

"I don't have a quick answer for that, but I'll talk to you after school. I hear my bus coming."

"All right. I have to walk to my building. Bye."

"Bye."

When Justin got on the bus and it pulled off, Julie teleported to outside the school building. Julie's school is very close to her home, so she walks to school every day. Since she was running late, she teleported there instead of walking. When Julie walked into the lobby, she ran into Mrs. C.

"Hello, Julie," Mrs. C said.

"Hi, Mrs. C," Julie replied. Julie was about to walk out of the lobby, but then she stopped. She turned

on her heel back toward Mrs. C. "Mrs. C?" Julie said.
"Yes?" Mrs. C asked.

"Thank you for partnering me up with Lia and Alex," Julie told her.

"You're welcome. I reckon the project went well?" Mrs. C asked.

Julie looked at her ring. "Yeah, it definitely did," Julie said.

20

Best Friends Forever

Julie found Lia and Alex in the hallway once she got to school. "Hey, guys. I had a really weird dream last night," Julie said.

"So did we! Was it about some school?" Lia asked.

"Yeah!" Julie said.

"Was it in the middle of nowhere?" Alex asked.

"Yeah!" Julie said again.

"Did it say 'Extraordinary Academy' in big letters on the school building?" Lia asked.

"Yeah!" Julie said again. "That's so weird that we all had the same exact dream," Alex said.

"Yeah," Julie and Lia both said.

Chapter 20

"I can't believe we only have a few months of school left here," Lia said, changing the subject.

"Me either. We have to start picking high schools soon," Alex added.

"In the dream, there was a school," Julie said.

"Yeah, but that wasn't real."

"But what if it was real? A few days ago, Justin was blabbing on about oneirology, which is the study of dreams. He told me that dreams are usually supposed to *mean* something. Maybe this dream is telling us that we might be going there soon," Julie said.

"The dream did seem kind of real," Lia said.

"OK, now you're just talking baloney. That dream was not real. But you know, if the dream wasn't real, which it wasn't, we're going to have to find a different high school to go to," Alex said.

"I hope we all go to a high school together. You guys are my first real friends, and I don't think I'm ready to say goodbye yet," Julie said.

"Yeah. I'm not ready to say goodbye either. If we don't end up going to the same high school, we've still got the rest of the school year and the entie summer to hang out," Lia said.

"We'll always be best friends," Alex said. They all hugged.

Crystie was standing at the end of the hallway watching them hug. She walked over to them. They all stopped hugging and watched Crystie as she walked over to them. "I'm glad you guys all became friends," she said to them.

"Thanks," Julie said.

"I'm sorry about all the drama I caused in your friendship."

"It's OK. You're forgiven," Julie said.

"Thanks. See you in class." Crystie walked away.

Julie turned back to Lia and Alex. "Crystie's right. I'm glad we all became friends," she said.

"Me too," Lia said.

"Me three," Alex said as they all walked to class together.

This isn't the end of our trio's story. Their adventure was just the beginning.

About the Author

Kayla Michelle Hebbon was born in 2003 and resides in New Jersey. Kayla has a deep passion for writing and wrote her first book at the age of 12. She also enjoys reading, drawing, singing, playing the piano, dancing, and hanging out with her friends and family. Kayla is very active in her community, where she has been a Girl Scout since she was five years old, participates in Jack and Jill of America, Inc., and is a proud member of the Somerset Chapter of the New Jersey Orators. Kayla has a great sense of humor and loves to make others smile. Her goal is to write many more books that will spark the imagination of those who read them.

CPSIA information can be obtained
at www.ICGtesting.com
Printed in the USA
BVHW03s1920080618
518619BV00007B/12/P

9 780998 776903